Pebble® Plus

Investigate the Seasons
Let's Look at Fall

by Sarah L. Schuette

Consulting Editor: Gail Saunders-Smith, PhD

Capstone press®

Mankato, Minnesota

Pebble Plus is published by Capstone Press,
151 Good Counsel Drive, P.O. Box 669, Mankato, Minnesota 56002.
www.capstonepress.com

1 2 3 4 5 6 12 11 10 09 08 07

Library of Congress Cataloging-in-Publication Data
Schuette, Sarah L., 1976–
    Let's look at fall / by Sarah L. Schuette.
    p. cm.—(Pebble plus. Investigate the seasons)
    Summary: "Simple text and photographs present what happens to the weather, animals, and plants in
fall"—Provided by publisher.
    Includes bibliographical references and index.
    ISBN-13: 978-0-7368-6705-4 (hardcover)
    ISBN-10: 0-7368-6705-8 (hardcover)
    1. Animal behavior—Juvenile literature. 2. Autumn—Juvenile literature. I. Title. II. Series.
QL753.S38 2007
508.2—dc22   2006020449

Editorial Credits
Martha E. H. Rustad, editor; Bobbi J. Wyss, set designer; Veronica Bianchini, book designer; Kara Birr,
    photo researcher; Scott Thoms, photo editor

Photo Credits
Corbis/Donna Disario, cover (background tree)
James P. Rowan, 21
Peter Arnold/Tom Vezo, 12–13
Photo Researchers, Inc/James Zipp, 7
PhotoEdit Inc./Dennis MacDonald, 18–19
Shutterstock/Alphonse Tran, 9; bora ucak, cover, 1 (magnifying glass); Elena Elisseeva, 5; Stuart Blyth, cover
    (leaf inset); Wesley Aston, 14–15
SuperStock/age fotostock, 11; Steve Vidler, 16–17
UNICORN Stock Photos/Robert Hitchman, 1 (rake)

The author dedicates this book to her Grandma Minnie Simcox of Belle Plaine, Minnesota.

Note to Parents and Teachers

The Investigate the Seasons set supports national science standards related to weather
and climate. This book describes and illustrates fall. The images support early readers
in understanding the text. The repetition of words and phrases helps early readers learn
new words. This book also introduces early readers to subject-specific vocabulary words,
which are defined in the Glossary section. Early readers may need assistance to read
some words and to use the Table of Contents, Glossary, Read More, Internet Sites, and
Index sections of the book.

Table of Contents

It's Fall 4

Animals in Fall 10

Plants in Fall 16

What's Next? 20

Glossary 22

Read More 23

Internet Sites 23

Index 24

It's Fall!

How do you know it's fall?

A cool breeze blows.

The weather is colder.

5

Leaves change color.

They flutter to the ground.

The sun sets earlier.

Fall days are shorter

than summer days.

Animals in Fall

What do animals do in fall?

Squirrels rush around.

They gather nuts

to store for winter.

Birds fly south.

They look

for warmer weather.

13

Bears search for a place
to hibernate.
Their fur coats grow thicker.

15

Plants in Fall

What happens

to plants in fall?

Ripe apples fill the orchard.

They're ready to be picked.

Corn ripens in the field.

It's ready to be harvested.

What's Next?

The temperature grows cold.

Fall is over.

What season is next?

Glossary

breeze—a gentle wind

flutter—to wave, flap, or float in a breeze; leaves flutter as they drop off tree branches.

harvest—to gather crops that are ready to be picked; fall is a time for harvesting crops such as corn, soybeans, wheat, and oats.

hibernate—to spend the winter in a deep sleep

orchard—a field or farm where fruit trees grow

ripen—to become ready to be picked

season—one of the four parts of the year; winter, spring, summer, and fall are seasons.

weather—the condition outdoors at a certain time and place; weather changes with each season.

Read More

Brimner, Larry Dane. *In the Fall.* Magic Door to Learning. Chanhassen, Minn.: Child's World, 2006.

Hall, Margaret. *Seasons of the Year.* Pebble Plus: Patterns in Nature. Mankato, Minn.: Capstone Press, 2007.

Latta, Sara L. *What Happens in Fall?* I Like the Seasons! Berkeley Heights, N.J.: Enslow, 2006.

Internet Sites

FactHound offers a safe, fun way to find Internet sites related to this book. All of the sites on FactHound have been researched by our staff.

Here's how:

1. Visit *www.facthound.com*

2. Choose your grade level.

3. Type in this book ID **0736867058** for age-appropriate sites. You may also browse subjects by clicking on letters, or by clicking on pictures and words.

4. Click on the **Fetch It** button.

FactHound will fetch the best sites for you!

Index

animals, 10, 12, 14

apples, 16

bears, 14

birds, 12

breeze, 4

cold, 4, 20

corn, 18

fur, 14

harvesting, 16, 18

hibernating, 14

leaves, 6

nuts, 10

orchard, 16

plants, 16, 18

ripe, 16, 18

sun, 8

temperature, 4, 12, 20

weather, 4, 12

Word Count: 106
Grade: 1
Early-Intervention Level: 14